Puffin Books

WHERE THE WHALES SING

'All she could recall clearly was the steady rocking motion that never stopped; the whales' song filling the grey-blue emptiness . . . and the encroaching cold. Always the cold . . .'

When Claire is stranded on the boat after her father is thrown overboard in a storm, she spends days and nights alone, her only solace being the whales that seem strangely to accompany and protect her, and their warm underwater world that beckons and soothes. But where are they going? And why is she caught up in their journey? As she drifts in and out of consciousness, Claire feels that something awaits her, some special purpose . . .

'. . . vividly evoked, immaculately polished and superbly paced. It shimmers and changes moods . . .

ra Times

'A mas   sitivity and fin

Reading Time

Also by Victor Kelleher

Forbidden Paths of Thual
The Hunting of Shadroth
Master of the Grove
Papio
Taronga
The Green Piper
The Makers
Baily's Bones
The Red King
Parkland
Earthsong
Fire Dancer
Brother Night
Del-Del
To the Dark Tower
Voices from the River
The Traveller
The Beast of Heaven
Em's Story
Wintering
Micky Darlin'

WHERE THE
WHALES SING

VICTOR KELLEHER

with illustrations by VIVIENNE GOODMAN

Puffin Books

Puffin Books
Penguin Books Australia Ltd
487 Maroondah Highway, PO Box 257
Ringwood, Victoria 3134, Australia
Penguin Books Ltd
Harmondsworth, Middlesex, England
Viking Penguin, A Division of Penguin Books USA Inc.
375 Hudson Street, New York, New York 10014, USA
Penguin Books Canada Limited
10 Alcorn Avenue, Toronto, Ontario, Canada M4V 3B2
Penguin Books (N.Z.) Ltd
182–190 Wairau Road, Auckland 10, New Zealand

First published by Penguin Books Australia, 1994
Published in Puffin, 1997
10 9 8 7 6 5 4 3 2 1
Copyright © Victor Kelleher, 1994
Illustrations Copyright © Vivienne Goodman, 1994

Typeset in Perpetua by Midland Typesetters, Maryborough, Victoria
Made and printed in Australia by Australian Print Group, Maryborough, Victoria

National Library of Australia
Cataloguing-in-Publication data:

Kelleher, Victor, 1939–   .
Where the whales sing.

ISBN 0 14 034493 4.

1. Whales – Juvenile fiction.
I. Goodman, Vivienne, 1961–   . II. Title.

A823.3

For Leila

V.K.

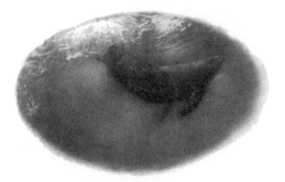

For my father

V.G.

I shall sleep, and move with the moving ships,
    Change as the winds change, veer in the tide.

                                    A. C. SWINBURNE,
                                    The Triumph of Time

CHAPTER ONE

Adrift

CLAIRE PEERED THROUGH the wind and rain, hoping for a better view. The boat, pitching and swaying beneath her, had ploughed down into a foam-streaked trough, so she had to bide her time. But as it rode up the next wave, the sail straining above her head, she saw it again: a jet-like spout of vapour shooting skywards; exactly the kind of spout made by the great humpback whales when they surfaced.

'There!' she cried, turning to her father who was standing in the cockpit beside her, both hands clenched about the wheel.

He brought his mouth close to her ear. 'Probably just spray,' he shouted. 'No good now anyway. Too rough.'

He was already turning the wheel, the sails rattling as the boat swung around and settled to a new course that would take them back to Sydney.

'But I saw it!' she insisted, shouting through the noise of the rising gale.

He shook his head, raindrops cascading from his chin and nose. 'Can't see anything in this,' he roared. 'Have to try again next year.'

Next year! The disappointment of it struck her more harshly than the wind. For weeks she had prepared for this trip; read everything she could about humpback whales; persuaded her father to give up a precious weekend's yacht-racing to bring her out here – all in the hope of sighting one of the migratory pods heading south for the summer. And here they were, beaten by the weather. With the dismal prospect of a whole year's waiting before they could try again.

'Please, Dad,' she began, 'can't we just look for a bit . . . ?'

She broke off as the boat suddenly bucked like a live animal. The violence of the movement hurled her from the cockpit and half-over the side. As she dangled there, held only by her safety harness, she spied a mountainous black shape curving past below. Then the boat was struck again, so hard that with a lurching roll it turned right over.

She realised what had happened even as she was dragged down. One of the whales she had glimpsed earlier had surfaced directly beneath them. She thought desperately: I'm going to drown! For black water was streaming past her face; more of it filling her mouth and nose, threatening to suffocate her. Struggling made no difference. The noise and the rush of water went on just the same. All she could do was hold on to the breath that was trying to burst out of her; keep her teeth clenched shut until, with another lurching tug, she was hauled up into the murky light and wind.

She found she was back in the cockpit again, standing knee-deep in water. The rest of the boat was in a state of ruin: the mast down; the mainsail, like the twisted, broken wing of a giant bird, floating alongside; the narrow decks running with water and half-buried under a tangle of wires and ropes.

'Dad!' she wailed.

And saw him immediately – his head and shoulders bobbing on a nearby swell of wave. He was struggling to reach the sail, but every stroke he took only seemed to draw him further away.

She tore the lifebelt from the side of the cockpit and threw it towards him, the way she had been taught. It would have been a good throw if it had not been for the wind, which lifted it and sent it careering off in the wrong direction.

The boat rolled sluggishly, as though about to turn over once again; and while she still had the chance she unclipped her harness, pulled open the hatch, and slid down into the cabin. There was water down there too, ankle-deep and cluttered with pots and pans that slopped noisily from side to side. Working hurriedly, and mainly by feel, she located the inflatable life-raft, stowed beneath one of the bunks, and heaved it up the ladder.

Her father was further away from the boat now, and downwind. He waved to her as she reappeared and shouted words she could not make out.

'It's all right, I'm coming!' she called back, and jerked the cord on the life-raft.

It inflated with unexpected speed. There was a sharp hiss of gas, and it squirmed like a living creature beneath her hands, growing magically into a canopied raft that was too large for the cockpit. She tried to steady it as it snapped out to its full extent, but the wind gusted strongly, spilling it over the side and tearing it from her grasp.

She seriously considered following it. Crouched at the stern, she readied herself to jump, hesitated, and finally held back – because the wind was spinning the raft away far more quickly than she could swim. Sitting high on the swells, it drifted straight towards her father. Thankfully, she saw him catch at its trailing rope and curl one arm over its inflated side; but before he could haul himself in under the canopy, a squall of rain swept down and he disappeared from view.

She could not believe at first what had happened to her. She, completely alone on a damaged boat in the middle of a storm! It was the kind of thing she had never even dreamed of; and for a while she stood there helpless, staring miserably through the billowing curtains of rain.

She was forced into action by the stinging impact of a wave breaking over her. Fully alert, she looked about her, assessing the situation.

Despite the water in the cabin, the boat itself was still riding well. What was hampering it, making it wallow dangerously in the troughs, was the shattered mast and rigging hanging over one side. If the boat were to survive, they had to be cut away; and with that in mind, she reached under the cockpit seat and detached the axe that was clipped there.

Closing the hatch, to keep out any more water, she crawled forward across the cabin roof. The wooden mast, she now saw, had snapped off fairly cleanly. Only some splinters of wood still attached it to its base, and these she chopped through with a few blows of the axe. Next, she set about disconnecting the thin steel cables that had held it in position. She was clinging to the rail when she undid the last of them, expecting the mast to slip easily over the side and float away. Instead, it swung towards her, knocking her down and crushing her leg hard against the rail post.

There was a tearing pain in her knee, so intense that for a few seconds she blacked out. When she came to, the mast was gone and another squall of rain was beating into her face. Grasping the heaving rail, she hauled herself up; but the slightest weight on her wounded leg made her feel sick and dizzy. Even the action of crawling back along the deck sent jabs of pain shooting up her thigh.

Huddled in the cockpit, shivering as much from shock and pain as from fear, she gazed forlornly out over the wind-tossed water, hoping for a glimpse of the life-raft. But all she saw through the drift of rain was a shiny black mound that might have been a whale, and might as easily have been a wave.

Dejected, fighting back tears, she re-opened the hatch. With the sail gone, there was no point in trying to steer. From now on the boat would follow its own course, regardless of anything she might do. Her only choice was to trust herself to the sea.

It was that thought which drove her below, as far as she could get from the black hillocks of water that loomed over the stern, as though about to topple down and crush her. Groaning because of the pain in her leg, she lowered herself into the cabin and closed the hatch behind her. In the darkness, water and unseen objects slopped around her feet. The wooden planking of the hull creaked and groaned. But loudest of all was the wind: like a lone wolf of the sea, it howled at the oncoming night.

In a feeble attempt to escape from it, she clambered onto one of the bunks and pulled a damp sleeping-bag over her head. It merely muffled the sound, reducing it to the voice of her own terror. She matched it with her sobbing cries; a faint whimpering that grew gradually softer and eventually stopped.

Oddly, for the boat continued to toss wildly to and fro, her sleep was deep and restful. Only once in the course of the night did she almost wake. For a minute or two the howling of the wind broke through the silence and entered her dream. Yet it failed to alarm her. In the dream, strangely, it mingled with the singing of whales: a low murmurous song that rose from the mysterious depths and whispered wordlessly to her of companionship and comfort.

CHAPTER TWO

Up from the Deep

CHINKS OF SUNLIGHT showed at the edges of the hatch; and the only sounds were the creaking of the boat and the slosh of water across the floor. Foolishly, she swung herself straight out of the bunk, causing the pain in her knee and thigh to return with a rush. Again she almost blacked out and had to cling onto the bunk to prevent herself from falling.

When her vision and her breathing steadied, she groped her way to the ladder, opened the hatch, and dragged herself up into the sunlight. Although the sea was still running high, the wind had dropped and the sky was a clear, uniform blue. As the boat drifted up onto one of the crests, she swept her eyes around the horizon, hoping for a sight of land or a glimpse of some passing vessel. But the white-capped sea was empty; and over to the west there was not even a smudge of grey to mark the Australian coastline.

She nearly started to cry again then and had to press her hands to her eyes to stop any tears escaping. They'll be looking for me by now, she told herself silently. In planes and boats and everything. They'll be sure to find me by nightfall.

She went on repeating that message to herself throughout the day. Sometimes she muttered the words aloud, to ward off loneliness and to keep her mind off the dull pain in her leg. For a while she believed so completely in what she was saying that she did not budge from the cockpit in case she missed some passing boat or plane. By mid afternoon, however, she was less sure; and she took time off to go below for a drink and to collect a tin of food from the emergency supplies.

The sea, meanwhile, had grown calmer, and for that reason much emptier. Back in the cockpit, eating beans from the tin, she was less eager to scan the horizon. There seemed little point. Also, she felt too hot to go on searching – far hotter than the spring sunshine warranted.

I must be sickening for something, she thought vaguely, and she peeled off her life-jacket and parka, stripping down to the lightweight wet-suit she wore beneath.

She had meant only to toss her discarded clothes onto the nearby seat, but somehow they slid over the stern and into the sea. Not that she really cared. The feverish heat in her body told her she would not need them again. Neither did she need any more to eat. She threw the tin aside and that also slipped over the stern.

As it sank through the sunlit depths, something moved towards it: a long sleek form that butted the strange object with its nose before spiralling upwards. A glistening grey arc broke the surface, like a perfect miniature of the great whale body she had glimpsed beneath the boat during the storm. And abruptly a whole school of dolphins was playing around the boat. Leaping and diving, they cut zigzag paths across each other's wakes, leaving behind a thin tracery of bubbles that glittered and shone.

Somewhere in the coolness of the waning day, she could hear someone laughing; and she guessed it was herself, glad not to be alone any longer.

Then, just as suddenly as the dolphins had arrived, they

were gone, and it was late evening, merging into night. Habit told her she should go below, lie down on the bunk and sleep. And she truly believed that was what she had done – until she woke from a dream in the middle of the night and discovered she was still lying in the open, her body bathed in sweat.

In the dream she had been swimming amongst the dolphins, their round eyes watching her curiously as she dived with them down into the blue depths, the sea cool and soothing on her bare skin. By contrast, the night felt hot and sticky, the watchful stars much less friendly than her animal companions. So she quickly closed her eyes and willed herself back into the dream, leaving the loneliness and discomfort of the waking world far behind.

She was not sure when she next woke. The painful throbbing in her leg returned and she sat up and looked out across a sea as flat and smooth as a lake. The sun was high, beating down mercilessly, the atmosphere stiflingly hot, as was she. There was no sign of the dolphins. The only movement was in the sea immediately around the boat, where she could detect the constant swirls and eddies of an ocean current that was bearing her towards the south. But why there? she wondered hazily.

For no reason that she could explain, she recalled how the humpback whale had risen beneath her, as though using its great body to buffet the boat off course, away from the land. It had been replaced by its dolphin cousins, their much smaller bodies swimming easily in and out of her dreams. She shook her head in confusion. Had they also been directing her, she asked herself, and should she follow?

Just asking the question was enough. It wasn't like being at home, with parents advising her or ordering her about. Here, there was only the windless day, the air grown furnace-hot, clinging to her skin like flame. And in response to the unbearable heat, she leaned out over the side.

Within arm's reach the sea glittered enticingly, as if urging her on; but as a precaution she took a short coil of rope from beneath the cockpit, tied one end to a stern-post, and flung the other end into the sea. Before she followed it, she paused briefly, amazed at her own audacity. Then she was plunging straight down into the placid blue of another world, exactly as in the dream. And as in the dream, all the unbearable heat left her body. Even the pain in her leg dissolved away, leaving her free to twist and turn as she pleased.

High above, she could see the rope, a thin white tentacle trailing behind the boat. The sight of it aroused an earlier fear, of being left behind, abandoned, and she shot hastily to the surface. But to her relief she found that the current was bearing her along too; she and the boat drifting southwards together.

She ceased to worry after that. Like the boat, she gave

herself to the ocean, satisfied by its silky cool touch. For what seemed to be hours, she swam lazily to and fro or dived deep; sinking down to where the sunlight barely reached and she was surrounded by soft darkness, her ears filled with the sound of her own heartbeat.

It was during one of these dives that she first became aware of an icy chill welling up from the depths. She shivered and stared into the formless gloom. At the limits of her vision she could see something moving: a large shadowy body swimming as lazily as she. Yet watchful, and drawing always nearer.

She recognised instantly what it was. The sleek head, the jutting dorsal fin, could have belonged to only one creature. A shark! Again she was caught in an upsurge of icy water that made her whole body shake with cold, and she turned in panic and arrowed up towards the boat hovering there in the calm blue of the day.

Always, during previous dives, the boat had remained floating above her, as if waiting. Yet now, while she was still struggling to reach the surface, it began drifting away, drawn on by the warm current, leaving her in the clutches of this much colder water that had lured the shark from the depths.

With silver bubbles billowing from her mouth, she kicked out desperately, fearful that at any moment the toothed mouth would snatch at her legs. The surface rushed to meet her and she burst free. Out into an ocean much wider and emptier than she remembered. A desolate blue waste in which she was no more than a tiny speck. Frantically, she swung around, searching. The boat was already out of reach, but the end of the rope was still swishing past, and she lunged and caught it with both hands.

As she was tugged along, half-buried in a smother of foam, she glimpsed the shark from the corner of her eye, its dorsal fin cutting the water over to her right. Purposely, she jack-knifed her body, driving herself under; and through a froth of bubbles and sun-streaked water, she saw the streamlined body swimming parallel to her own. Idly flicking its tail, it veered in towards her, one expressionless eye observing her coldly as it slid beneath her exposed belly and half-turned.

'No!' she screamed out, not to the air and sky, but to the vast watery spaces of the ocean. 'Get away!'

Her cries seemed to go no further than herself; to be swallowed up by the blue-black emptiness. And again the shark was sliding beneath her, its rough sandpaper skin rasping against her legs as it passed. Shuddering from the contact, she surfaced long enough to gulp in air and then jack-knifed down once more, convinced that if she took her eyes off the creature for more than a few seconds it would strike.

The rope was biting into her palms now, her arms and shoulders aching from the effort of holding on. There was also the cold to contend with, her limbs growing stiff and unresponsive. So that when the shark angled in for the third time, she could not kick out in self-defence, even though it slowed as it brushed against her: its body as icy cold as the surrounding water; its tail slapping her aside with cruel playfulness.

'Help me,' she murmured softly, as if pleading with the ocean itself. 'Please make it go away.'

The only response, more heartless even than the silence, was the appearance of another dark shape swimming up from the deep. It was bigger than the shark – longer, far bulkier – and moving with strangely ponderous speed.

This new danger was more than she could bear. Choked with terror, she clawed at the rope, lost her grip entirely, and surfaced in a flurry of foam.

Immediately the shark closed in, its dorsal fin cutting a straight, deadly line through the water. But before it could reach her, something glittered and broke far beneath them – a succession of bubbles that exploded from the dark shape swimming below and spun upwards. The bubbles reached the surface in long thin lines, like strings of silvery beads; a curtain of them that formed a protective circle around her helpless body.

Although that enclosing circle was made of nothing but air, the shark was unwilling to enter it. As it halted its rush and slanted away, several smaller shapes followed the ascending bubbles. Their tails pumping energetically, they drove at the shark, scaring it off; their beak-like mouths issuing excited, clicking cries as they leaped gracefully from the water.

Claire felt one of the bodies rise gently beneath her, its skin unexpectedly warm, reassuring. Just as gently, it bore her across the surface towards the boat and floated there while she reached up with trembling hands and gripped the side.

Only when she was safely on board did she fully realise what had happened. And by then the dolphins, their job done, had disappeared. The bulky shape far below had also gone, back into the darkness from which it had come. Though she knew it now for what it was: not a shark at all, but a great whale, the air from its lungs forming the net of bubbles that had saved her.

Perhaps because she had read about those glittering circles of bubbles, she was not surprised. 'Thank you,' she whispered through chattering teeth. And with her chilled body pressed against the hot planking, she drifted back into unconsciousness.

CHAPTER THREE

Riding the Whale

STILL HALF-ASLEEP, she could sense the whales down in the darkness. She knew, too, that beyond the shadowy pink of her closed eyelids, out there in the bright day, their massive backs would be breaking the surface of the ocean, their spouts misting the sunlight. One of them must have risen close to the boat, because she felt a cool wash of spray on her fevered skin. So refreshing that she could not resist it; and despite the persistent pain in her leg, which made her moan aloud each time she moved, she hauled herself up onto the stern.

The whale, a fully grown humpback, was still floating alongside: its body a shiny black hillock; its flippers, immensely long and knobbly on the front edge, like giant oars jutting from its body. It rolled half onto its side for a better view of her, one huge low-set eye regarding her with a strange air of understanding. As though in sympathy with what it saw – her face and neck badly sunburned and blistered – it blew again: the spray, smelling of the sea and its many tiny creatures, drifting over her as before.

'Yes!' she gasped. 'Yes!' And lifted her face thankfully to the fine mist.

Beside her, the eye, the long head and body, submerged in a welter of foam. The vast black-and-white flukes were all that remained, poised above the surface; and then they too descended, thwacking the water so hard that the resulting wave drenched her.

She had no need to make any conscious decision. Like the water running from her hair and skin, she slipped easily over the stern and into the blissfully cool embrace of the sea. It accepted her as if she were no longer a creature of the earth, the silvery surface closing over her head, the whale's turbulent wake drawing her down.

Some way ahead, through the sun-dappled blue, a blurred shape was swimming with a slow undulating motion. It grew still as she strained towards it, floating there in the watery space, waiting patiently. She closed the gap with a few strokes, diving beneath the tail to where the white undersides were blotched with barnacles and fragments of trailing weed. Further along, from the middle of the belly to the extent of the thrusting jaw, the whitened skin was ridged with even lines of pleats – long grooves pressed into the pale flesh. Wonderingly she reached up to touch them.

But that was testing the animal's patience too far, and with a shuddering roll it flicked her with one of its long side-flippers. There was no aggression in the action. It was the gentlest of movements, yet still she was sent tumbling down and down to where the sunlight ended and the blackness began.

Below her, the murky heart of the ocean waited, more watchful than ever. On this occasion no sinister shapes circled in the shadows; no icy water gusted up to where she hovered. Even so, she did not care to linger there.

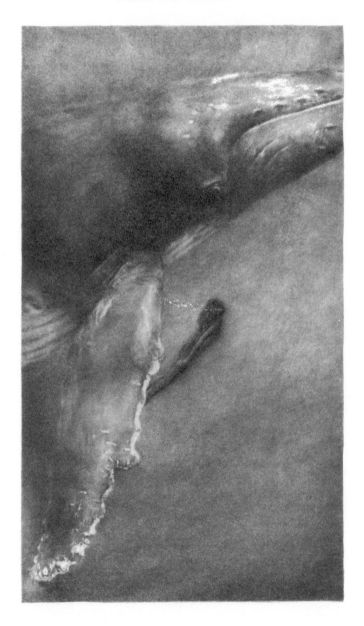

The memory of the shark was too fresh. And she turned and kicked upwards, filling her aching lungs with fresh clean air as she broke clear.

By her own calculation she could not have been under for more than a minute or so; but in that time the day had been transformed. A sharp wind had sprung up, the beginnings of a swell already appearing; while overhead the blue sky was giving way to a haze of cloud.

The suddenness of the change was enough in itself to alarm her, and she looked around for the boat. It was no longer close by. Driven by the wind, it was nearly a hundred metres away, its bows dipping into the low swell.

As with her encounter with the shark, she nearly panicked. Instead of conserving her energy, she began thrashing at the water in a frantic attempt to close the gap.

And close it she did, surprisingly quickly. For as she soon realised, the boat was not being pushed forward by the wind. It had merely been blown sideways, she and the boat still held by the strong current, both of them still being carried southwards at the same rate.

Relieved, she trod water while she caught her breath. And now that she was calm, she saw something else that reassured her. The whales had not left: their spouts, like friendly signals, jetted skywards on every side. Wherever she looked, mountainous backs curved into view. She was swimming in the very midst of the pod which was also heading south, keeping pace with the boat.

One of the whales passed almost beneath her, the wash sucking her under. Another much smaller shape followed: a calf swimming in its mother's wake. Unlike the mother, it checked its forward movement at the sight of her: its long-jawed head lifting to where she hung in the clear blue; its eyes gleaming through the pale light, as if in recognition. When it seemed that the giant face must collide with hers, it swerved slightly and, as inquisitive as any puppy, drifted past so close that one of the piebald flippers brushed her arm.

This brief contact was an invitation that she accepted readily, stretching out with both hands and grasping the knobbly edge of the flipper. The young animal did not quiver or shy away as the adult whale had done earlier. There was an eerie, inviting cry from the mother, calling the calf to her side, and all at once Claire was being dragged forward, the flipper softly pulsing beneath her hands.

A few seconds later the calf surfaced for air. As well as filling her own lungs, Claire used the opportunity to transfer her grip to the small dorsal fin on the animal's back. In that position, half-lying, half-sitting astride the broad body, she was swept under once again.

They went deeper than before, to the brink of the darkness that she usually feared. Though not now. Not with the mother's cries reaching them from above, calling them back up. Obedient but unhurried, the calf rose through lightening shades of blue to where the wind was whipping the tops from newly formed waves and the sky had grown leaden-grey.

Gulping in more air, she had to suppress a shiver, as though this world of wind and low cloud were really what she needed to fear. Then they were plunging back into the calm of a sea whose soft blue folds preserved the vanished warmth of the day.

For some time after that they rose and sank with a rhythm that Claire found peculiarly comforting; she and the calf snatching breaths at the same regular intervals; their heartbeats, like their bodies, attuned to each other. The periods up there in the day, where the wind sang across the boat's hull, were so brief that soon she found she could almost ignore them. The rest, the slow movement through the moist underworld, gradually took on the likeness of a dream, of a long sleep, in which the pain in her leg faded away, as did the lingering fever-heat of her body, leaving her with a sense of peace and silence.

Only one sound penetrated the silence: the mother whale's inviting voice, high-pitched, calling to her calf each time they sounded. Always it responded with a faint bleat of its own and with a brief surging motion. Except for once, when the mother's cry was a little more urgent, a little more insistent. The change in the tone was so slight that Claire failed to notice it. But the calf registered the difference immediately, and instead of swimming up to the mother's tail, it dived beneath the protective bulk of her body, searching for the nipple.

The next cry to reach them spoke so clearly of alarm that even Claire realised something was amiss. Low and booming, it came from some distance away – from a whale swimming on the outer fringes of the pod. And without hesitation both mother and calf plummeted in a steep dive, dragging Claire with them.

She was rushing through darkness, her head threatening to burst from the increased pressure, before she had the presence of mind to let go. High, high above, like a tiny silver-grey circle at the far end of a tunnel, she could see the sky. She climbed towards it, thrusting aside the thick water, following the trail of gleaming bubbles that leaked from her mouth and raced on ahead. In the last few metres she almost caught up with them. Her body shooting up and slicing through the mirror-surface . . . to where someone else was already waiting, watching for her appearance!

She saw the figure as she was drawing in her first gasping breath. Someone more or less her own size, floating between her and the boat. The head and shoulders, like her own, bobbed above the surface; the face, no less startled than hers, stared wide-eyed back at her.

'Who . . . ?' she half-shouted, and realised it was not a person at all, but a seal; and that its round eyes were not just startled, but glazed with terror.

That brief act of recognition was all she had time for. One moment the seal was there; the next, it was swallowed up in a great eruption of water. In its place there was a much larger head and shoulders: a tooth-rimmed mouth still gaping; a powerful, neckless torso, with precise black-and-white colouring, outlined against the sky.

Her recognition of this other creature was instantaneous.

'Orca!' she breathed out – using the name she had seen printed in books, beneath illustrations of killer whales.

The creature crashed sideways back into the water, sending out a ripple of wavelets that reached to where she floated. Others of its kind were swimming near by, their dorsal fins speeding across the surface.

She did not try and escape. If the seal had simply given up and waited for death, what chance did she have? She, who had none of the seal's swimming skills; who was trapped here, near the surface, by her constant need for air – the same air that now struck cold upon her cheeks and neck.

Some of that unfeeling cold seemed to invade the surrounding sea, and she glimpsed another black-and-white shape hurtling up from below. There was no time for terror. She felt a sickening lurch of dread as she braced herself for the sheer force of the impact. And a split-second later the danger had come and gone. Instead of a cruel

26

and bloody mouth erupting where she had once been, there was a gentle parting of the waters close beside her; a bullet head angling from the surface; an open mouth, with a huge tongue lolling against the lower rim of dagger-teeth, as if the orca were laughing at her – sharing with her the pleasure of its discovery that she was not a seal, there simply to be eaten. Its orca mind fascinated by her slender limbs and her helplessness, and also by a mysterious sense of fellow-feeling.

It uttered a few clicking cries, and one of its companions rose beneath her and buoyed her up on its blunt forehead. She balanced there as the orca swam, head held high, through the heaving swell to where the rest of the pack waited. It released her then and, nervously to begin with, she swam amongst them, nudged this way and that by the tender pressure of their large bodies. A baby, hardly longer than herself, mouthed her arm with teeth that could easily have sheared through her soft flesh; yet it left behind only the faintest pattern of toothmarks that quickly faded. She tried to follow it as it swam away, but she was too slow. And too cold and tired – her time in the water and her recent shock starting to take their toll.

Over to her right the boat continued its slow drift, bows to the wind, and she began swimming towards it. Several of the orcas, thinking she was confused, nudged her around, pointing her back towards the southern horizon where the cloud hung especially low and steel-grey. But when she insisted on turning aside, they seemed to grasp her purpose. One of them (the one that had lifted her earlier?) butted her forward, half-raising her from the water, pushing her along.

For the orca, their progress must have been slow. To Claire – a miniature bow-wave riding up her chest and splashing into her face – it felt as if they were racing along. The boat rushed to meet them, dropping into a trough as they approached, so they were almost level with the rail. A casual toss of the orca's head was all that was needed, and she was pitched over the rail and down into the cockpit.

When she rose and looked out, the whole pack had gathered about the boat, heads up, mouths agape as if in laughter. She wanted to join in, despite the desolate wastes of ocean all around; but the wind was too cold, like ice on her exposed skin, and she huddled down.

She did not hear them swim away. Nor, when she peered over the rail and found them gone, did she feel abandoned.

In her tired, fuddled state, it was as if the boat itself had taken on the likeness of a whale – she clinging to its back as it rode the swells; sucking in her breath each time it teetered on a crest. Even the wind had become a familiar voice, calling to her, beckoning her southwards.

CHAPTER FOUR

A Debt Repaid

SHE DID NOT want to take refuge in the cabin. It wasn't just the water and debris washing about the floor that worried her, but the darkness, which reminded her too vividly of the ocean depths where the sun never reached. On the other hand, up there in the cockpit it had become bitterly cold. And with her parka and the rest of her clothes gone, she finally gave in and went below. Though not to stay. Only to refill her water-bottle and to change into a thicker wet-suit kept stored in one of the lockers.

It hurt her leg changing wet-suits, and she had to bite her lip so as not to cry out. Yet the thicker rubbery material did give some support to her damaged knee, and she was soon much warmer, even comfortable enough to sleep.

At least she thought she had been asleep, for when she

opened her eyes she felt rested, and the humpback whales had returned. She could hear their singing just by pressing her ear to the decking. Their voices, mingling with the wind that howled around the boat, spoke to her of contentment, even of joy.

With difficulty, her body strangely weak out there in the light and air, she grasped the side rail and sat up. The sea, like the sky, had turned from blue to steel-grey; and the low swells had grown into steeply sloping walls of water that foamed and boiled along their crests. In these cold, colourless wastes, there seemed to be no place for life and warmth, and she almost huddled back down. What held her there was the sudden appearance of an albatross, riding the storm with carefree abandon. Its long wings tipped trustingly to the wind, it slid over the nearest crest and banked sharply, its breast feathers only a hand's breadth from the water as it swooped along the inward curve of the trough. She glimpsed its eyes as it sailed past, so clear and bright, so devoid of fear; eyes that found nothing alien about these wild surroundings.

The whales were the same, totally at home here. Not just swimming, but frolicking in the rough seas; the spent air exploding from their lungs as if in triumph; their bodies, shiny black, filled with untold energy, heaving clear of the grey water in an open display of joy.

Even the boat showed every sign of belonging in these waters. It was dancing ahead of each breaking crest and dropping abruptly to where its bows plunged into the grey swell – only to shake itself free, with water pouring from its decks, and climb easily back into the wind. Again and again it emerged from the deep sea valleys unscathed, its up-and-down motion so familiar that when a whale rose alongside, Claire automatically loosened her hold on the rail and slipped into the sea.

There, at that moment, it somehow felt the natural thing for her to do. To move from the chill, noisy region of the wind into the warm silence of the waves; to abandon the flimsy shell of the boat, a thing of wood and metal, and choose instead a creature of flesh and blood.

And this time the whale accepted her completely. A faint shudder passed through it as she clung hard to its dorsal fin, but that was all. Its blow-hole winked shut and it pitched forward into the advancing swell, parting the waters so cleanly that Claire felt the merest tug. Then she was moving once more through a world of stillness, where the only sounds were the eerie voices of the whales calling to each other.

Above her, the long slopes of the waves drifted past, the boiling crests like blossoms of cloud in an otherwise silver sky. Angling upwards, they broke briefly through that sky, out into noise and confusion, and descended again, back to where peace reigned.

Another whale moved up from the lower realms of shadow and she transferred her grip – kicking free of one giant body and fastening herself to another. It also accepted her presence, letting out a lowing cry of welcome; each upward lift of its tail bringing their bodies into momentary contact.

She could see other whales now: bulky shapes that glided with surprising grace through the gloom ahead. Whenever one drew near, she would swim towards it, her arms outstretched. And always her newly chosen companion would slow down and wait, floating patiently until it felt her hands tighten about its dorsal fin.

She was left behind only once, when she lost her grip and slipped back, the beating of the giant tail tossing her towards the surface. But she was not abandoned there for long. Before the crest of the next wave could reach her, there was a moaning call, half of welcome, half distress, and a heavily barnacled head lifted her clear. For a second or two she actually stood on the flat upper jaw. She took several quick steps backwards and was swept off her feet by the rush of water. But by then she was secure again, her hands clamped around the dorsal fin as the wave passed harmlessly above them.

She had no idea how long she had been swimming when she spied the calf. She heard its squealing cry, high and joyful, and it came hurrying towards her, its chunky body pumping vigorously. The mother, as always, was hovering in the background, her white underside faintly luminous in the poor light that fell like a blue-grey curtain to where they swam. She called to them, urging them higher, as Claire wrapped her legs around the calf's body and held on tightly.

It was as well that she did, for the young animal, overjoyed at this unexpected reunion, began cavorting wildly – twisting and diving, breaching in a flurry of spray and surfing down the long swells.

Because of the rush of water past her ears, Claire could hear the mother only faintly, her distant, mewing cries half-lost in the excitement of the moment. That was why the initial alarm went unnoticed. The first inkling she had that something was amiss was when the calf suddenly jerked and slewed around. The low voices of the bulls were booming out by then, warning of danger.

Claire, clinging on still, glanced nervously about her. The surface waters, which only minutes earlier had been thronged with vast blurry shapes, had become abruptly empty. Unnervingly so. The stillness no longer peaceful, but filled with nameless threat. Of all the humpback pod, only one adult remained in view: the mother, a brush-stroke of shadow far below, calling to them plaintively.

A tremor shook the calf's body and it dipped its head and drove downwards. But even before Claire could relax her hold, another dark form passed between them and the mother. A killer whale, the distinctive white markings reflecting the dim light.

Their escape route cut off, the calf lunged for the

surface – but other killer whales already waited there, black silhouettes against the silver sky. More of them patrolled on every side, circling slowly.

Entirely surrounded, the calf grew unnaturally still – Claire continuing to crouch on its back. They were both watching one orca in particular: a large male that was steadily closing in. Her lungs bursting, Claire longed to float free, to rise up to where she could suck in the cold, life-giving air; but she knew that if she deserted the calf now, it would be dead in seconds.

It was almost a relief when the orca began its charge, coming at them in a fast, shallow curve, its mouth open, ready to tear flesh from bone. She had only an instant in which to act, and quickly she threw back her head and let out a wordless shriek. The bubbles gushing from her mouth obscured her vision momentarily, so she did not see the way the orca balked at the sight of her – the sudden image of her limbs twined about the calf's mottled body causing it to check its charge and skim away. She glimpsed it passing over her shoulder, one pectoral fin brushing her cheek. And then she was pulling at the calf, urging it to rise.

Luckily, they surfaced in the calm water at the very base of a trough. With the calf blowing beside her, her first desperate gasp took in more steam than air. But as her breathing steadied, she noted with approval that the orcas showed no sign of renewing their attack. They were still circling dangerously, but holding off while she remained with the calf.

Encouraged, she took an extra-deep breath and bore down on the calf's head. It responded half-heartedly, too stupefied with fright to do more than duck beneath the oncoming wave. Again she leaned forward and pushed at the flattened upper jaw: and this time it began to swim down sluggishly. Several of the orcas accompanied them for a while, peeling off one by one as they sank deeper. At the point where the light gave way to blackness, only one big male remained, the last of their dangerous escort. Her head almost splitting from the pressure, Claire watched him also spiral away. Though still she hung on, wanting to be sure that the calf was truly safe.

Go! she kept urging it silently, for its movements remained sluggish. Go!

In answer to her voiceless pleading, a mewing cry sounded from the deep. And with one powerful thrust of its tail, the calf broke Claire's grip and vanished.

She was left floundering in the blackness, her head throbbing so violently from the pressure that she no longer knew which way was up and which was down. Slowly, more sluggish than the petrified calf, she groped her way through the gloom. Magically, it seemed, a light appeared before her, but too dim and distant ever to be reached. It was better, perhaps, to go on drifting here, on this borderline between day and night.

She had almost stopped swimming when the orcas arrived. Twirling about her, the slight pressure of their bodies jostling her into wakefulness, they bore her upwards. She neither helped nor resisted them, her arms too slack and weak to fend them off even had she wanted to. Through half-closed eyes, she could see the light expanding, brightening; but the darkness within her was stronger, drawing her to itself much as the mother whale had enticed her young.

She retained no memory of reaching the surface; nor of clambering back into the boat. When she awoke it was night, the sky clear and black and speckled with stars. The wind blew as fiercely as ever, shrieking insanely as it buffeted the tiny boat, heaving it from side to side. In all that noise and motion, it was impossible for any other voice to reach her. Yet now, without needing to be told, she understood why she was there. She, like the whales, was caught up in a great journey to the southern oceans. Where something awaited her. Some special purpose that . . .

But again she slept.

CHAPTER FIVE

Intruder

SHE MUST HAVE been ill for a while. Waking and sleeping fitfully, she was vaguely aware of days passing and of the boat driving on beneath her. Sometimes, half-awake, she would hear the whales calling far below, their melodious voices oddly in keeping with the moan of the wind and the gurgle of water along the sides. Even asleep she was conscious of their distant song, the long wailing notes reaching her through a haze of darkness and mist.

That same mist continued to shroud the day when she finally recovered. It was light, but with no sign of the sun. The sky was an oppressive roof of cloud that glowed dully. Lower portions of cloud, like flimsy strips of muslin or lace, were peeling away and curling lazily past the boat, so that often she felt as if she were adrift in the sky. Only the thrusting motion, as the boat scurried down the long swells, reminded her of where she truly was: the surrounding sea as limitless as ever; the following waves still mountainously high. Though now that the wind had slackened, the tops of the crests were softly rounded and no longer ridged with foam.

Listlessly, she reached for the water-bottle and was surprised to find it empty, for her lips were cracked and dry and caked with salt. She was equally surprised to find how weak she had grown. She had to make several attempts just to stand up; and the climb down into the cabin, to refill the bottle, was almost beyond her.

Back in the cockpit, the musty taste of stored water easing the soreness in her throat, she rested for a while before clambering onto the stern. That also taxed her strength. Yet it was worth the effort, because she felt better, stronger, the moment she released her hold and rolled sideways into the welcoming sea.

Compared with the clammy touch of the mist, the sea was warm. And unlike the deck, it was soft, exerting a gentle upward pressure that supported her full weight. Floating free, one hand holding lightly to the trailing rope, she could feel her lost strength returning; the contained energy of the waves somehow flowing into her limbs, healing her.

At her first dive, she saw the calf: a familiar mottled shape waiting patiently beneath the waves. She tried to copy its mewing cry as it hurried to meet her – and may

well have been successful, because when the mother
loomed out of the background dark, she showed no hint
of nervousness; her barnacle-encrusted snout nuzzling
them both lovingly.

As before, Claire was soon drawn into the communal
life of the pod. In company with the calf – sometimes
clinging to its fin, sometimes swimming unaided – she
moved easily amongst the great rising and dipping bodies.
The way the adults watched her with their large soulful
eyes, so trustingly, made her feel as if she were also a calf.
Their snoring sighs, their repetitive song, might have been
aimed directly at her, like some previously unknown
language she was rapidly learning to understand. Certain
sounds she recognised as offering encouragement; others
as expressing care and concern; others again, more strident
and demanding, obviously warned of danger.

It was a series of such warning cries that sent her
shooting to the surface; the rest of the pod diving deep,
down into that icy darkness she dared not enter.

As she had suspected, the orcas were the cause of the
alarm: their angled fins, their piebald backs, clearly visible
near the crest of the oncoming wave. But this time it was
not the humpbacks they were after. Far up the opposite
side of the same wave there was a flash and glitter of darting
bodies. Seals! Fleeing desperately from the hunters.

Infected by the fever of the hunt, the orcas spared her
only a brief greeting as they sped past. She barely had time

to return their greeting before they disappeared, leaving her alone.

Alone, but not lonely. Because she knew that the whales would soon be back. Also, some inner sense warned her that for the time being at least the calf was safe. In the immediate future it was not the orcas it needed to fear, but . . . But what?

She shivered, suddenly unsure, and reached for the rope trailing in the water near by. Looping it about her waist, she let it drag her slowly along; calmed, lulled almost into a state of sleep, by the steady movement. Content to drift on until she was startled into alertness by the horn-like calls of the adult humpbacks; and the squat outline of the calf reappeared beneath her, matching its body movements to hers.

She rejoined it eagerly, sinking down into the friendly half-lit area beneath the waves. The two of them swimming together as if nothing had happened to disturb them. The calf's smooth body pressed warmly against her own.

Yet not warmly enough. For every so often she was overtaken by a fresh fit of shivering – the cold coming not from below, but filtering down from above. The glittering surface like a sheet of ice that made her gasp every time they broke through; the air knife-sharp on her wet skin, cutting into her lungs with each breath.

More than ever she was thankful to duck back down; preferring to hold her breath until she was dizzy rather than urge the calf up to where the light shone icily upon the sleek banks of passing waves. And with practice she found she could stay down for longer and longer periods, as if her body were accustoming itself to this watery underworld.

How long she swam with the calf she was never sure. Hours? Days? Even afterwards, looking back, it was hard for her to estimate the exact time. All she could recall clearly was the steady rocking motion that never stopped; the whales' song filling the grey-blue emptiness . . . and the encroaching cold. Always the cold. Numbing her flesh. Seeping into her bones. So that no matter how tightly she clung to the calf's warm young body, still she could not keep the deep chill at bay. Her limbs growing stiff with it; her teeth chattering until her jaw ached.

Eventually it was the cold that drove her back to the boat. Unable to hold on any longer, she floated free of the calf and rose helplessly. The animal followed for a while, calling sadly as it spiralled about her. Other, much larger whales, responding to its cries, slid from the shadows: giant creatures that watched her depart with an air of regret, their trumpeted song imploring her to stay. But she was too feeble now to do more than drift up to a surface that glinted like frosted glass.

She crashed through it in a shower of icy droplets. Out into a world more dreary than she could have imagined. Colourless and empty. The sky leaden; the sea, arched with waves, reflecting back the same drab greyness. The mist, much thicker than before, had become a drapery of dirty white lace torn into fragments by the breeze.

And there was something else about the day that worried her. Something she could not pin down at first – though it made her glance uncertainly across her shoulder as she reached for the rope and pulled herself wearily from the water. It came to her then – that there was also a sinister quality about this dismal scene. As if some dangerous, hidden presence were waiting out there, preparing to strike.

Half-kneeling in the cockpit – blue with cold, her shoulders hunched and shaking – she peered nervously over the side. The character of the sea, she discovered, had begun to change. The long waves were no longer smooth, their surface unbroken. Now, bobbing ice-floes were appearing in the slack water of the troughs. Their number increased steadily as the day wore on: some small; some almost as big as the boat. Towards nightfall a particularly large floe – an iceberg in miniature – sailed over the nearest swell and bore down upon her. Tall and jagged, it jarred against the boat, grating and shrieking its way along the gunnel and making her cringe down onto the deck.

When she looked up the mist had closed in. A hazy white curtain, it hovered just beyond her reach, deadening every sound, reducing the boat's forward momentum to a dreadful stillness from which she feared it would never break.

She waited, ill at ease, shaking now from more than the cold. At last, gratefully, she felt a slight breeze on her cheek, and straight away the curtain of mist was split in two. But through the ragged tear, she saw not light and space: only something more sinister still. The kind of intruder she had never dreamed of sighting here. A dark shape in silhouette. A low-hulled ship passing across the near horizon, the throb of its motor reaching her through the silence.

Again she cringed back, not even tempted to call out for help. Because that one glimpse, before the mist closed and hid her from view, had been enough. She knew beyond all question what she had seen. No ordinary ship, but a whaler. The unmistakable shape of a harpoon-gun perched right up on the bow.

Hastily, she pressed her ear to the deck and listened. The low song and the throb of the engine sounded together. As did her own broken sob of distress. She could not help herself; could not keep silent as she knew she should. All she could think of was how the whales, at that very instant, might be spearing up towards the dying light. The calf amongst them. Its mottled back brushing aside the ice-floes as it surfaced. While near at hand the whaler lay in wait, its harpoon-gun trained upon the sea.

CHAPTER SIX

Journey's End

W<small>AKING WAS HARDER</small> than usual. Like struggling up through ice-bound water towards a ring of frosty light. Groggily, her eyes still clouded with sleep, she emerged at last into a raw wintry day. Windless. The sea unnaturally calm. The air hazy with half-frozen mist. Through the mist, she could make out the blurred outline of vast phantom shapes. Icebergs. Some so tall that they towered above her, their peaks lost in cloud. In contrast to their ghostly whiteness, the stretches of open sea were dark blue merging into black, and mirror-smooth.

It was through that glassy smoothness, without warning, that a whale breached. A giant male humpback, it burst joyously through the surface, scattering water in mirror-fragments as it shot skywards. At its highest, the tip of its thrusting snout rivalled the icy peaks, all but its flukes clear of the water. With a sound like a gunshot, it blew

noisily, shattering the silence; and its great body, as it fell back, stirred the placid sea into foam and sent waves shuddering away.

Claire had barely recovered from her surprise when another adult male breached even closer to the boat, its whole body twisting in a kind of joyful dance before it flopped back. Within minutes that same dazzling display was repeated again and again as one male after another drove up vertically through the misty air and pirouetted upon its tail, its oar-like fins twirling freely.

All around the boat the sea was boiling and foaming. The boat had begun to rock wildly, as if it too were celebrating the whales' arrival at their feeding grounds. And Claire, looking on, had to cling to the handrail to prevent herself being flung against the sides of the cockpit.

Then, as suddenly as it had started, the display was over, and the whole pod settled to the business of feasting on the swarms of krill that populated these southern waters. Instead of breaching enthusiastically, they were now diving deep and releasing rings of bubbles that rose to the surface like circular nets in which countless tiny creatures milled about. The whales followed close behind: their cavernous mouths gulping in huge quantities of krill; the unwanted water pouring out through their massive jaw plates.

Like the whales, Claire was so caught up by their activity that for a while she was aware of nothing else. What first alerted her to possible danger was a vague suggestion of movement somewhere out there in the mist. It was accompanied by a low hum that grew ever louder and became eventually the unmistakable throb of an engine.

She saw it then, for the second time: the dark outline of the whaler! The thing she had longed never to meet again; that she had hoped was merely a part of some bad dream. For surely whalers no longer existed. Surely! Wasn't that what she had read in books? In magazines? Yet there it was, passing across the narrow channel between two icebergs. As black as they were white, but no less ghostly. More hungry than any orca and far more deadly.

It was visible only for the space of a few breaths. She blinked and it was already fading, nosing its way back into the grey-white pall of mist. Though now she no longer doubted its reality. It was out there still, circling the peacefully feeding pod. She had only to turn her head to hear it: the throb of its engines like the beating of some heart of steel.

'Go away!' she screamed. And then, to the whales that continued to feed, unafraid: 'Leave me!' Because she preferred to be abandoned, left alone in all that cold wasteland, rather than have them fall to the harpoon.

But although her voice carried shrill and clear through the still air, it could not penetrate down through the glassy surface of the sea, to the swarming dark where the whales swam contentedly.

49

Again the whaler appeared, over to her right – a lean, wolfish look about its low-slung shape; its jutting prow armed not with teeth, but with the sinister shape of a mounted gun. She swung towards it; glimpsed a human figure on the prow; a human face peering intently along the gunsights. Never had she seen a face so unfeeling, eyes so empty of warmth. And she opened her mouth to protest, but once more the veil of mist drifted back, the ship and its harpooner fading to nothing.

She realised then that she had little time in which to act. The whales had to be warned. Painfully, because the ache in her leg had returned, she dragged herself up onto the stern, swung her feet over the edge . . . and stopped! She had been expecting to find the water cold, but not like this! So icy that it seemed to burn the skin of her bare feet, to penetrate instantly through the lower half of her wet-suit and chill her to the bone.

She knew she could not last long in such a temperature. A few minutes of full alertness was all she could hope for. After that, weakened, overcome by drowsiness, she would begin the slow drift into . . . No, not sleep. She understood well enough what awaited her down there. Hadn't she already encountered the shark, its lean body knifing up through waters as icy as these?

Instinctively, she drew her legs clear and pulled herself back on board. And it was then, while she was kneeling

on the stern, undecided, that the whaler made its third
and final appearance.

Some sixth sense warned her of its presence even before
she heard it. The throbbing pain in her leg and the throb
of the engine suddenly became one and the same. Behind
her the mist parted, torn aside by an unseen hand: and
there, coming straight towards her, was the knife-edge of
the ship's prow. Above it stood the loaded gun; and above
that again, the cold-eyed face staring past her.

She stumbled clumsily to her feet and began waving her
arms frantically, but the harpooner seemed not to notice
her. His eyes were fixed hungrily on the waters ahead, upon
a scene she somehow knew by heart, without needing to
turn and look – the blue-black surface of the ocean divided
by the glistening arch of the female whale's body; and in
her wake, within sight of the harpooner, the mottled,
defenceless back of the calf.

This time Claire did not hesitate, entering the water in
a long clean dive. The first shock of contact drove the
breath from her lungs, forcing her up. Desperately, willing
her freezing muscles to obey, she sucked in more air and
dived again. The water all about her was murky with
krill – thousands of the tiny creatures, like dust motes
dancing in the dim light, which made it impossible to see
more than a few metres ahead. But behind her the churning
power of the engines was growing more distinct, and she

clawed at the shadows that hemmed her in; heaved with numb hands and arms until a much larger, moving shadow appeared out of the gloom.

The calf, as always, greeted her with a squeal of delight. She tried to answer it with a warning; but in her half-frozen condition she could manage no more than a feeble croak, the breath leaving her mouth in a slow dribble of bubbles. Already beginning to weaken, she grabbed for a side-fin and squirmed onto the animal's back; and the calf, thinking she was being playful, shot towards the surface.

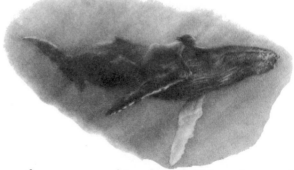

It was the very worst thing that could have happened, because the mother immediately followed. All three of them marooned there in the bleak Antarctic day, with the whaler bearing down upon them.

From the corner of her eye, Claire glimpsed the man swinging the gun into position, steadying it for the shot. All her instincts demanded that she leap clear and save herself. Yet somehow she could not bring herself to do it. Why had she come here, she wondered briefly, if not for this? And to her own fearful astonishment, she stood up on the calf's flattened snout, placing her trembling body in the direct path of the harpoon.

She had barely straightened up when she heard the muffled crack of the harpoon being fired. It was accompanied by a yell as the man yanked at the gun, jerking the muzzle high in a frantic attempt to avoid hitting her. But with her eyes clenched shut, from sheer terror, she knew nothing of that. There was a whistle of something passing above her head; the whine and twang of heavy rope racing out; and then a dull boom as the head of the harpoon exploded harmlessly somewhere beneath the surface.

What saddened her afterwards was that she never had a chance to say goodbye. No sooner had the explosion sounded than the calf fell away from beneath her – both calf and mother dropping like stones into the safety of the depths. She was left floundering, while the whaler swept past, the turbulence of its wake sucking her under.

That nearly finished her, the violence of the undercurrents sapping her strength, drawing her down to where she lacked the will to resist. Entombed in the black krill-heavy sea, the cold like an iron clamp upon her lungs, she came close to losing her grip on that slender thread of belief that connected her to this place. With her heart labouring on in the darkness, she might almost have been anywhere – even closed up in the sightless regions of her own mind: an inner world that offered no easy escape;

where she could wander deeper and deeper, until the silence and the gloom became complete.

Yet if she was the one who had saved the calf, finally it was the calf that saved her. She never forgot that, in spite of all that people said later. For it was the calf's plaintive call, no one else's, which rose from the ocean floor and broke in upon her isolation: the young animal voice, like a bright light of sound, pointing her upwards; directing her through the maze of confusion and doubt, up to where the long Antarctic day lingered on.

She was only half-conscious when she surfaced. The whaler by then had disappeared, swallowed for ever by the mist. Feebly, past caring what happened to her, she swam back to the boat. Her limbs numb with cold, she dragged herself over the stern and into the cockpit.

Lying there, gazing up, she watched as the tall blue-white icebergs drifted past. The slow procession told her that the boat was moving again, caught up in the same current that had already brought her so far. At the thought of her journey continuing, a warm ray of hope entered her frozen body. It occurred to her that she might yet catch up with the whales and ride free on the back of the calf as she had before. There, where the southern ocean ended and all journeys began anew, she and the whales might . . .

Her one faint hope was destroyed a moment later, when the boat, after lurching noisily from side to side, came to a jarring halt. The impact pitched her half-way down the companionway and she had to crawl back. That was surprisingly easy, because the boat was now lying on its beam, having run aground on a flat shelf at the base of one of the icebergs.

Still shaking with cold, she grasped the side rail and lowered herself onto the ice. Above her rose a blue-white cliff that glistened and shone even in that misty atmosphere. So this, she thought calmly, is where it all ends. Here, in a shimmering ice-world.

Half-crawling, she made her way up a snowy incline and sat with her back to the cliff. From there, she had a wide view of the ocean. It appeared bluer than she remembered it. The mist had lifted, and while she watched, the clouds thinned, parted, and the sun filtered through, unexpectedly warm on her face. There was a stir of movement beneath the sea: high triangular fins, rounded at the top, were cutting cleanly through the water; hooped piebald backs disrupted the mirror-surface. She smiled and waved a greeting, gladdened by the way the orcas raised their voices in reply, piping happily as they sped past.

Satisfied at last, she leaned back and closed her eyes, giving herself to the sun's warmth and to the drowsiness that crept like slow flame through her chilled body. The last thing she heard as she fell asleep were the farewell cries of the orcas. Then she was plummeting, not into blackness, but into sun-streaked depths of unbroken dream, where the great whale shapes resumed their song and the calf swam joyfully from the shadows.

CHAPTER SEVEN

Saved

THE SUN WAS still warm on her face; but it was shining now through an open window whose silky white curtains were being lifted idly by the wind. She turned and saw a long room filled with beds, and it dawned on her that she was in a hospital. Someone was sitting close beside her, holding her hand; someone else bending over her pillow.

'She's coming round!' she heard her father say in an excited whisper.

And her mother's face, smiling with relief, dipped down towards her.

That was how she found out she had been saved. Though not until the next day did she feel strong enough to tell her story.

Propped up in bed, her broken leg encased in plaster, she described to her parents all that had happened –

starting with how she had cut away the mast and ending with the boat running aground on the ice. She left nothing out.

When she had finished, there was an embarrassed silence. Her mother coughed uncomfortably and looked out of the window.

'I know you think you're telling us the truth,' her father said gently. 'But really it couldn't have been like that, believe me. You just imagined it. You see, the chances are you were never more than a hundred kilometres from land. They found the boat washed up on the south coast. You'd managed to crawl ashore and were lying unconscious at the base of a cliff.'

The image of a tall, shimmering cliff of ice came back to her quite vividly, and she shook her head. 'No, it really happened,' she insisted. 'I was there, swimming with the whales. I saw it all. The shark and the calf and the whaling ship and . . . and everything.'

Her mother coughed again. 'You only *thought* you saw those things,' she murmured unhappily. 'You were delirious, that's all.'

'Delirious?'

'It was because you stayed in the open cockpit,' her father explained quickly. 'You suffered badly from exposure. There was the pain from your broken leg as well. Most of the time you wouldn't have known where you were.'

She felt too tired to go on arguing with them. What

would have been the use anyway? As far as she could tell, their minds were made up. According to her father, even something as solid and real as the whaling ship had to be an illusion. After all, hadn't the nations of the world given up whaling years before? There was also the problem of the icebergs: they only existed in Antarctic waters, far from where she had actually been. Or so he claimed.

'You might as well face up to it,' her mother concluded in a kindly voice. 'It all took place inside your head. Nowhere else. It was a wonderful dream, but a dream just the same. The kind of thing that sometimes happens to people in a high fever.'

Claire nodded, saying nothing, acting as if she were convinced. And she went on acting like that not only for the rest of the afternoon, but during their subsequent visits. As the days slipped by, it seemed so much easier simply to pretend that her parents were right; far easier than trying to answer all their objections. So that by the end of a week, when she was well enough to go home, it was more or less assumed that she had come round to their way of thinking.

'How's our whale girl today?' her mother asked jokingly when she arrived to collect her.

With a nurse's help, Claire eased herself from the bed down into a wheelchair. She was so glad to be leaving the hospital that she didn't mind being made fun of.

'Oh, about ready for another journey to the South Pole,' she answered.

They were still laughing together when her father drove up to meet them at the hospital entrance. She had not seen him for a couple of days and his face appeared unusually serious.

'So what are we waiting for?' her mother prompted him once Claire was settled comfortably in the back seat. 'Let's go home.'

He hesitated, one hand resting uncertainly on the ignition key, his eyes seeking out Claire's in the rear-view mirror.

'I've been down the coast to pick up the boat,' he explained. 'There are a few things that have me puzzled.'

'Is that a reason for sitting here outside the hospital?' her mother began laughingly. But then, noticing his expression, she grew equally serious. 'What is it?' she asked.

'Well, the boat was a bit of a wreck, as you'd imagine, but it was still intact. And it had a rope where Claire said it would: trailing from the stern-post. Exactly what you'd need if you were in the sea and wanted to climb back on board.' He paused and drew in his breath. 'I discovered something else as well. When they found Claire, she was wearing a heavy-duty wet-suit. They hadn't mentioned that before. Evidently it was stiff with salt. As though . . . as though she'd spent a lot of time in the water.'

'In the water?' her mother echoed him sharply. 'You mean swimming? But surely you don't . . .'

'Hold on,' he interrupted her, 'there's one last thing. Half an hour ago, before I came to pick you up, I rang Greenpeace. I was told there are still whaling ships. They're referred to as research vessels these days, but the fact is they still hunt whales.'

He swung around now and gazed straight at Claire. Her mother had also turned towards her. Both of them obviously troubled, doubtful, looking to their daughter for reassurance.

Once again she felt tempted to tell them what had actually happened. Then, all at once, she realised that there was no need to. Somehow it was sufficient just to know the truth; to be sure in her own mind of all that she had seen and done. Hadn't she shared the great southward journey of the humpback whales? One of the greatest journeys in the world? Wasn't that enough in itself?

She gave a deliberate shrug and lowered her eyes. 'It's like you said,' she answered dutifully. 'I was delirious most of the time. I probably didn't have a clue about what was going on while I was out there in the boat.'

Yet that was not what she was thinking at all. Secretly, she was reliving her days and nights at sea: picturing to herself the bulky shapes of humpback whales gliding gracefully through the blue; hearing again the calf's last squealing call, an urgent voice directing her away from the blackness of doubt and disbelief, up towards the brightening day.

She blinked in the strong sunlight streaming through the side window of the car, suddenly aware of krill-like specks of dust floating in the air all about her.

'Yes,' she breathed contentedly. 'Anything could have happened while I was out there. Anything . . .'

About the author

With a host of award-winning novels to his credit, Victor Kelleher remains one of Australia's most celebrated writers for both adults and children. Born in London, he lived in Africa for twenty years before moving to New Zealand where he began to write, prompted by homesickness for Africa. He moved to Australia in 1976.

Victor's first book for young people was *Forbidden Paths of Thual* and since then his novels have received many awards and commendations. His prizes have included the Australian Children's Book of the Year Award and the Australian Science Fiction Achievement Award. More recently, *Parkland* was shortlisted for the 1995 Australian Children's Book of the Year Award. Formerly an associate professor, he now writes full time.

About the illustrator

Vivienne Goodman was born in Christchurch, New Zealand and moved to South Australia when she was six. She graduated from the South Australian School of Design in 1982 with a degree in illustration. Shortly after, she completed her first picture book, *Oodoolay* by Robin Klein, and has also illustrated the picture book *Guess What?* by Mem Fox. Vivienne has produced some of the most well-known and highly acclaimed cover images for children's books. She lives in Adelaide, South Australia and is a full-time illustrator.